Maisie goes to a Wedding

Maisie goes to a Wedding

Author and illustrator Aileen Paterson

GLOWWORM BOOKS LTD

This story is dedicated to
Angus and Caitlin Taylor,
Amelia Young, Anna Lancry-Beaumont,
Johnny and Maisie Harley,
Katherine Fraser, Eleanor Scott,
and Jennie Paterson Brown.

Thanks to Mark Blackadder

© Aileen Paterson

First Published in 2000 by:
Glowworm Books Ltd. Unit 7, Greendykes Industrial Estate,
Broxburn, West Lothian, EH52 6WY, Scotland

Telephone: 01506-857570
Fax: 01506-858100
E-mail: admin@glowwormbooks.co.uk
URL: http://www.glowwormbooks.co.uk

ISBN 1 871512 54 9

Printed and bound by Scotprint, Musselburgh

Designed by Mark Blackadder

Reprint Code   10   9   8   7   6   5   4   3   2   1

Other Maisie titles in the Series:

Maisie and the Space Invader   *Maisie and the Posties*
Maisie's Festival Adventure   *Maisie goes to School*
Maisie goes to Hospital   *Maisie loves Paris*
What Maisie did Next   *Maisie in the Rainforest*
Maisie and the Puffer   *Maisie goes to Hollywood*
Maisie Digs Up the Past   *Maisie and the Pirates*
Maisie's Merry Christmas

One morning Peter the Postie delivered exciting news to all at Number 13 Morningside Mansions in Edinburgh. Every cat in every flat received an invitation to a wedding. It was going to be the biggest wedding of the year.

Caitlin Catflapp was getting married to Angus Furrbelow!

Angus was a very famous footballer . . .

HE PLAYED FOR SCOTLAND.

Pernickety panloaf Mrs McKitty purred with delight. "A wedding invitation. Absolutely excellent!" she told her budgie, Billy. "I simply must buy a new hat!"

"ANOTHER HAT! Imagine that," cried Billy. No wonder.

Mrs McKitty already owned ninety-two hats! They attracted attention wherever she went.

Next door, Maisie's granny was thrilled to get such happy news. She was Caitlin Catflapp's favourite aunty, and Caitlin had asked her to make the wedding cake. It was all very exciting.

Granny didn't know it yet, but there would be a few UPS and DOWNS on the way to the big day . . .

There were a few ups and downs that afternoon when Maisie and her friend Archie got home from school. When they heard the news they weren't nearly as pleased as Granny and Mrs McKitty. They had much more exciting news of their own!

"I'm afraid we can't go to the wedding," said Maisie. "That's the day our football team has it's big match against the London Lioncubs. We're going to WEMBLEY! Archie is our best striker, and, guess what, I've been picked to be goalie!"

"Blethers! Of course you will go to the wedding!" thundered Mrs McKitty.

"Oh no we won't," cried the kittens.

"Oh yes you will!"

"Oh no we won't,"

"Oh yes you jolly well will! This wedding is far more important than a silly football match for kittens."

The kittens were very annoyed. Their tails swished angrily. Their school team was top of the league and the Lioncubs were the cream of the English teams.

Oh dear, thought Granny, Mrs McKitty fairly knows how to put cats' backs up.

"I'm so sorry, but you'll have to miss your big game," she said.

"We can't let Caitlin down. She would like you two to be her bridesmaid and page. Now, won't that be nice?" Archie and Maisie didn't think so.

They spent the rest of the afternoon up in their tree house, moaning and groaning.

"What happens at weddings anyway?" asked Archie.

"I don't know," sighed Maisie. "I think everyone gets dressed up in fancy clothes. I don't LIKE frilly frocks. I don't want to be a bridesmaid. I want to be a goalie!"

"And I HATE frilly shirts," growled Archie. "I was really looking forward to that match. It's so unfair!"

Soon there was more for them to complain about. If there was one thing Archie did not enjoy, it was shopping. Now that he was to be a page, his mummy took him shopping every day to look at silly trousers and frilly shirts. Poor Archie.

Maisie didn't like shopping very much but it was better than getting measured for her bridesmaid's dress.

She felt very gloomy.

Her daddy was far away on an expedition, exploring in a jungle where there were no posties or telephone boxes. Poor Maisie.

To make matters worse, Spotty Wilson and Curly Pow had taken their places in the football team.

"DRAT THIS WEDDING!" cried the kittens.

There was so much to do and so little time that no one noticed the two grumpylumps up in the tree house. They were all up to their ears and whiskers in wedding plans. Peter the Postie was delivering piles of wedding presents. Caitlin was busy trying on wedding dresses. Angus was busy training and trying on wedding suits. Miss Betty Braw, the dressmaker, was sewing dozens of fancy frocks. Granny and Mrs McKitty were hard at work in the kitchen. Pounds of flour, bags of sugar, cupfuls of fruit and spices had to be measured and mixed with butter, eggs and milk. It was going to be a very special wedding cake. They stirred the mixture in two big bowls then poured it into two giant cake tins and popped them into Granny's oven.

Unlike Maisie and Archie, Granny and Mrs McKitty LOVED shopping. They had been so busy they hadn't had time to do any. As soon as the wedding cake was baked and cooling in the kitchen, they got ready to go to town to look for new hats and posh frocks. They felt very chirpy as they set out . . . but more ups and downs were on the way . . .

First of all they visited hat shops and tried on lots of hats.

Granny couldn't find any that suited her. They all made her look like a Granny Mushroom!

Mrs McKitty only found one that tickled her fancy. She was just about to buy it when she bumped into Miss Gingersnapp — wearing one exactly the same. Goodness Gracious that would NEVER do.

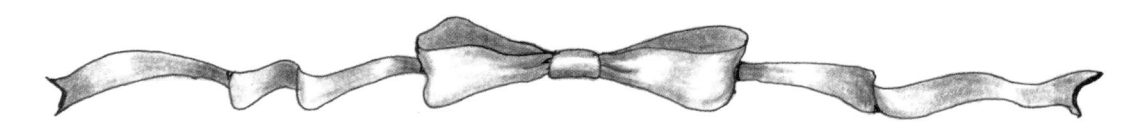

They decided to try on frocks. This time they were in luck. They saw lots of lovely ones. There was only one problem . . . None of them fitted! Buttons popped. Zips wouldn't zip up. Too many puddings and pies had made them podgy.

"I'm very sorry madam," said the shop assistant, "but this is our largest size. Perhaps you should try our Roly-Poly department on the third floor."

Mrs McKitty didn't like this idea at all.

"THE ROLY-POLY DEPARTMENT!! No thank you," she sniffed.

"Dearie me, Marjorie," said Granny "What are we to do?"

"There is only one thing to do. We must go on a diet, immediately!"

They jumped onto the 23 bus and rushed home to join The Morningside Slimcats Club.

Every afternoon they went to Keep Fit class.

It was hard work!

So was the Slimcat diet!

(Too much lettuce. Not a lot of Sticky Toffee pudding.)

Soon they were as grumpy as the kittens.

"No more cream cookies," sighed Granny.

"No more chocolate biscuits," sighed Mrs McKitty. "I'm fading away."

"DRAT THIS DIET!" they cried.

The weeks flew by. Soon there were only a few days left before the wedding. Peter the Postie was glad. His bag was light again. Angus had finished his training and Caitlin had found a lovely wedding dress. The wedding cake was ready to be decorated. Granny and Mrs McKitty covered it with creamy icing and roses and ribbons. It looked beautiful. It made them feel very hungry!

There wasn't much time left. Now that they were a wee bit slimmer, and a lot fitter, they set off to visit the shops again. This time they were lucky. They found frocks that were the cat's whiskers and hats that were the bee's knees. They even found something for Billy to wear!

Now it was time for Maisie and Archie to try their wedding clothes. Miss Braw, the dressmaker, delivered the bridesmaid frock in a big box. Granny lifted it out and slipped it over Maisie's head. It was made of silk, the colour of bluebells.

Before Maisie had time to look in the mirror the doorbell rang and Archie appeared. He was wearing a new kilt and a plain white shirt.

"My, you look nice, Maisie," he said.

"So do you. Is that what you're wearing to the wedding?"

"Yes. I took my Mummy shopping for a change and we found just what I wanted."

"NO FRILLS!" laughed the kittens.

Billy the budgie wasn't laughing when he saw what he was to wear to the wedding. He got a shock when he looked in his mirror.

"GADZOOKS!" he squawked.

"I look a Right Silly Billy. DRAT THIS HAT!"

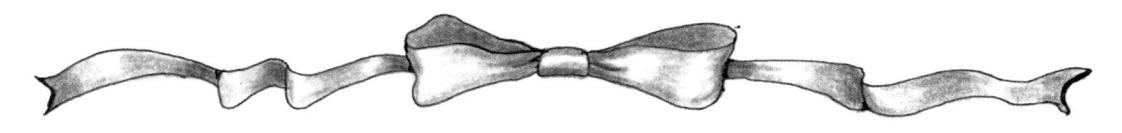

The ups and downs were over.

Cats were on their way to Edinburgh from far and near . . .

Mr Catnipp, Maisie's millionaire friend, was whirling in from Brazil . . .

. . . Aunty Tibbie was zooming up from Somerset . . .

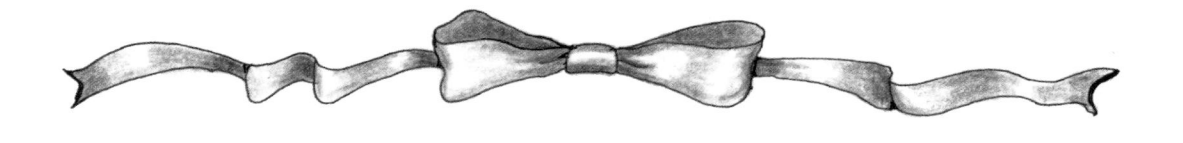

. . . Uncle Sandy and his crew were steaming along in their Puffer . . .

THE NIPPY SWEETIE

...A bus full of passengers was leaving London...

... Cousins were motoring over from Deepest Glasgow ...

... The Californian Clan were flying in on a jet plane ...

... The French mice, Alphonse and Mimi Mousse, were driving, toot sweet, all the way from Paris ... and many more ...

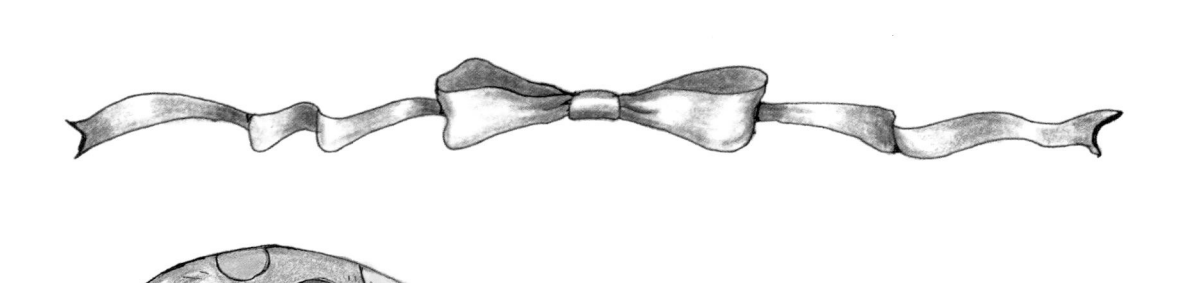

Last of all, and best of all, on the morning of the wedding a big balloon blew in from Borneo and parked in Maisie's backgreen, next to the tree house.

DADDY HAD COME HOME!!
He was just in time!

The kittens rushed out to meet him. He gave Maisie a hug.

"Hello my wee cough drop," he said "My word, you and Archie look splendid. A pair of bobbydazzlers!"

What a lovely surprise for Maisie!

The wedding was a lovely surprise too. She and Archie enjoyed *every minute*.

They did their jobs perfectly and they didn't get any pawmarks on Caitlin's long white dress. The church was crowded with all their friends and relations. Mind you, Mrs McKitty's hat took up quite a lot of space by itself. It was a corker . . . the biggest hat in Scotland. Mrs McKitty was very happy. Angus and Caitlin were very happy too, and Granny was so happy she cried into her hankie. Daddy took photographs of everyone outside the church and Angus threw silver pennies to the kittens waiting there.

After that there was a PARTY at the Caledonian Hotel!

First of all, there was wonderful food to eat. Smoked salmon . . .
prawn cocktails . . . lobster tarts . . . chicken pies . . . and haggis.

When Granny and Mrs McKitty saw all the nice things they
forgot all about their diet. They had three helpings of trifle!

There was cheesecake for the mice and seedcake for Billy, but
the wedding cake was the most delicious of all.

There were speeches and then there was dancing . . .

Fur was flying and kilts were waggling as cats flew round the
floor. There were tangos and fandangos, and jigs and reels.

Mrs McKitty danced the Gay Gordons with the minister!
Mr Catnipp and Aunty Betty and Uncle Al taught everyone how
to do American dancing.

Well, not quite everyone . . . Some cats were missing . . .

They were in the hotel garden playing *football*!

What a match! It was just as fast and furious as the dancing indoors. The chef and the waiters were there . . . Daddy, Angus, the bridegroom . . . and Maisie and Archie.

MAISIE WAS GOALIE!

"I can't wait to tell everybody at school that I played football with Angus Furrbelow!" cried Archie.

"And I can't wait to tell Spotty Wilson that he didn't manage to get any goals past ME!" laughed Maisie.

It had been the biggest, best, wedding ever. (Not many weddings have a football match in the middle!) Maisie would never forget it. Everything had turned out fine after all and Daddy was home.

P.S. A few weeks later, Peter the Postie delivered more exciting news. This time it was for Maisie and Archie. Daddy was off on his travels again, but he had sent them a surprise present. Two tickets to see Angus playing for Scotland in The Cats World Cup Final . . .

SCOTLAND WON!

They beat BRAZIL!

And when Scotland went up to collect The Cats World Cup . . .

MAISIE AND ARCHIE WERE THERE!

GLOSSARY

wee	small
pernickety	fussy
blethers	nonsense
toot sweet	toute de suite/immediately
bobby dazzlers	smashers
corker	an excellent thing
panloaf	an affected way of speaking

TootalootheNoo